for my mother

pou

By William Wondriska

UNIVERSE

In a large freight yard, there once lived a small steam engine.

He was so small and was made so long ago that he could only

puff his way around the yard.

DINGDINGDINGDING

PUFF

Each day one of the big engines, on its way out of the yard, would speed

DING DING DING DING

past **PUFF** all alone in his corner. **PUFF** never left the freight yard.

PUFF would switch freight trains from one track to another,

but nothing important ever happened to him.

Out in the great world his little puff would hardly be heard at all,

unless he could run along the floor of a deep canyon

and then little **PUFF** would echo like this . . .

PUFF

PUFF

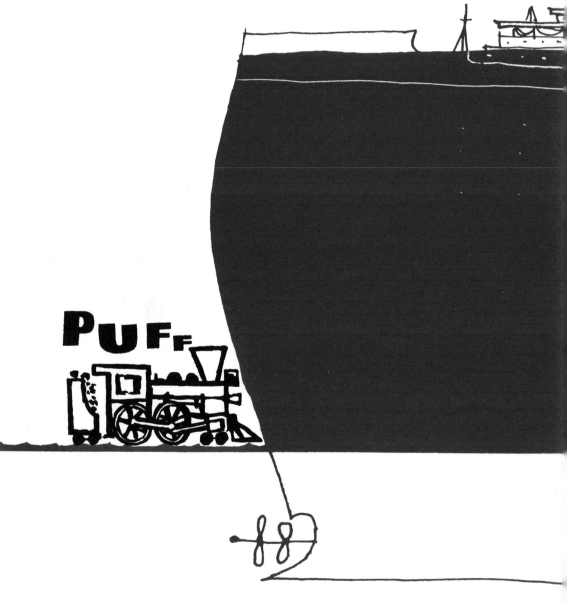

If only he could swim! Then he could push the huge ocean liner into

its place at the pier.

Or, if all the engines in the world were little **PUFF**s

P U F F F F

P U F F F

P U F PUFF

P U F F

P U F

P

they would be the ones to climb the highest mountains. It would not be easy going up

PUFF

but what fun it would be riding down!

PUFF might even travel to other countries. To Egypt

to Italy

to India

to France.

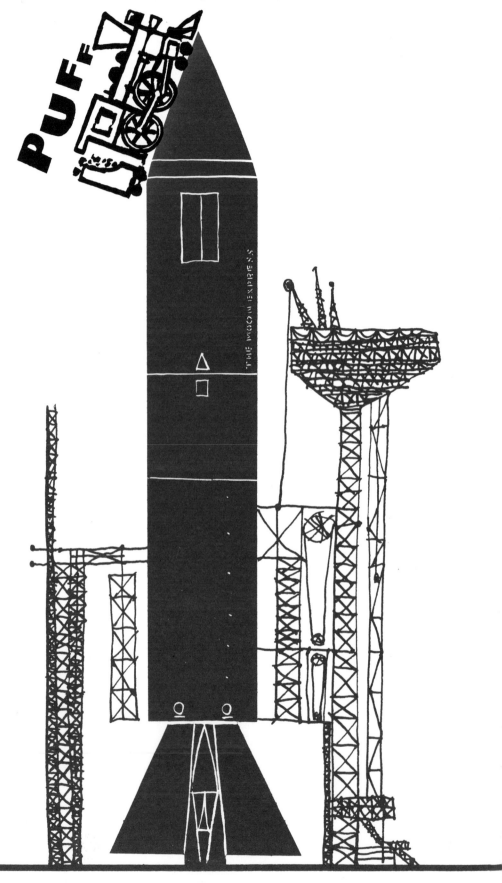

He might even be the first engine shot off a rocket into outer space!

But no, none of these things ever happened to little **PUFF**.

He was just a freight yard engine. Or he was, until one day when

it

began

to

snow

and snow . . .

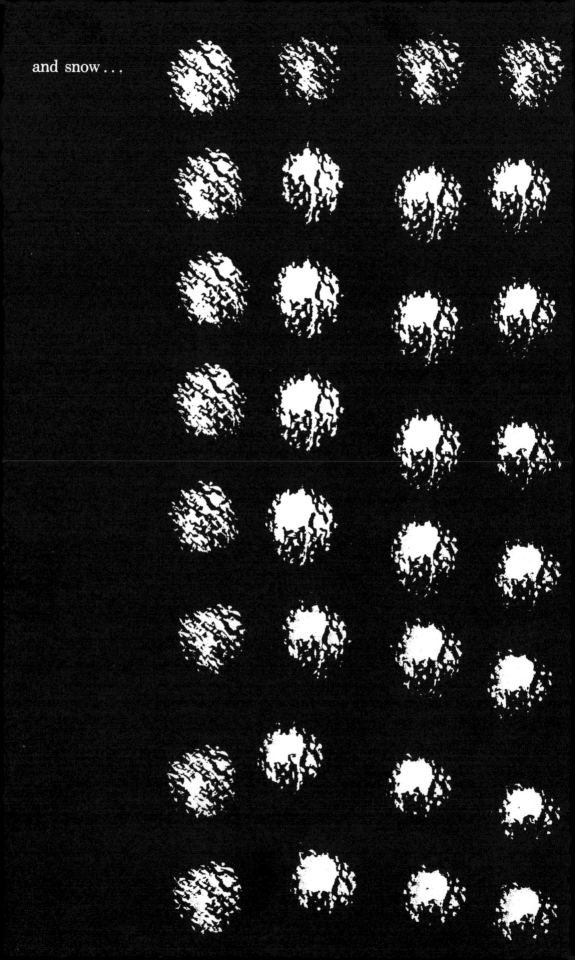

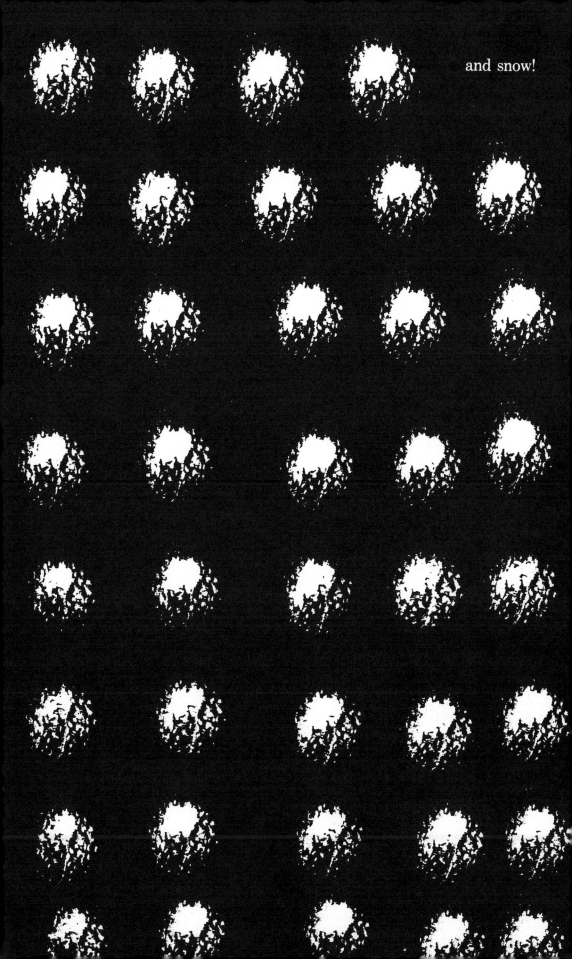

and snow!

Suddenly out of the blinding storm, a diesel engine came slowly

into the freight yard pulling a long line of circus cars. Snow had

seeped into the controls of the big engine; it would not run.

There was not a spare diesel in the whole yard. The animals were

wet and cold, and soon they began to howl and yowl and screech.

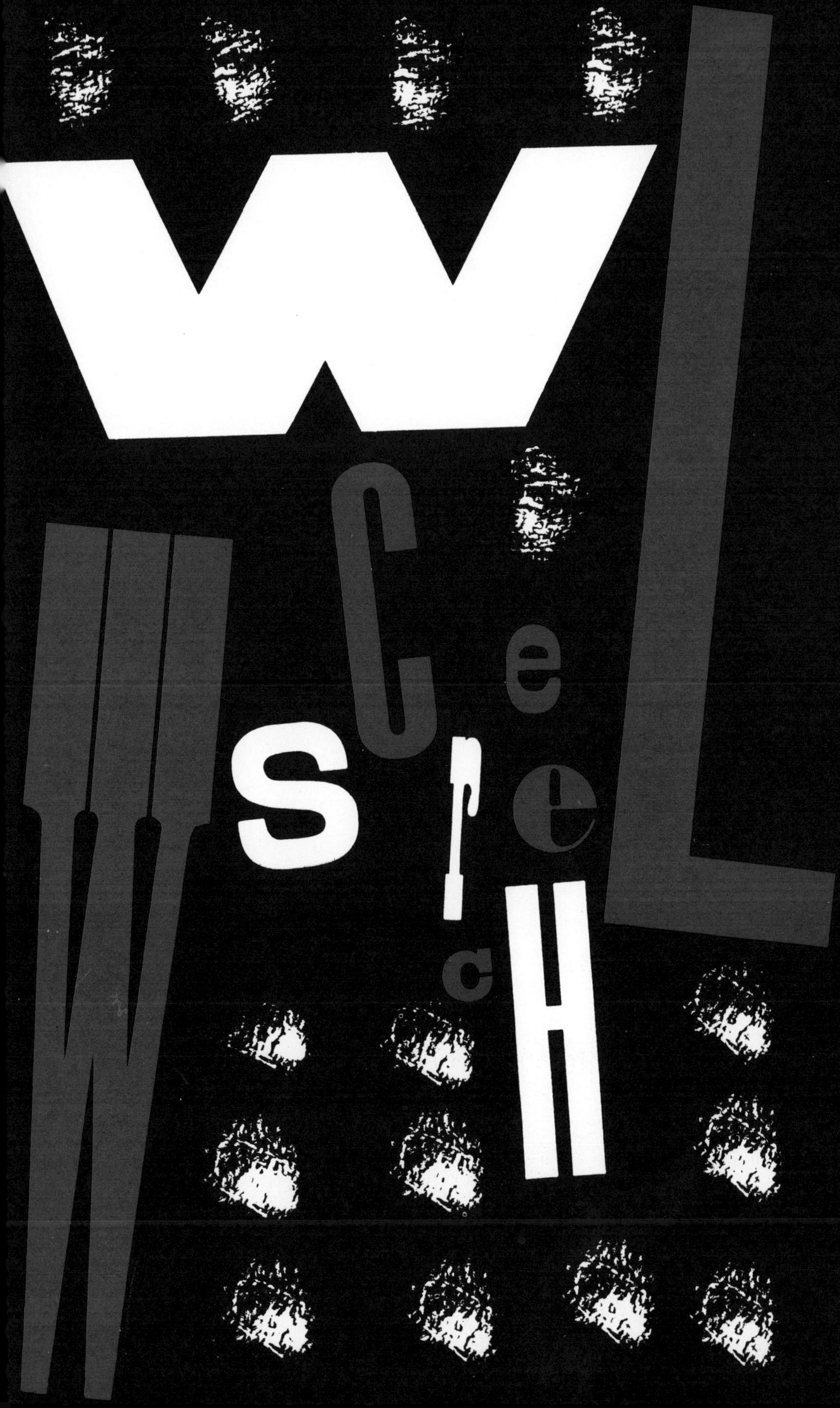

Something had to be done!

The diesel engine was towed to another track;

PUFF was hooked up to the circus train,

and away they rode, out of the storm.

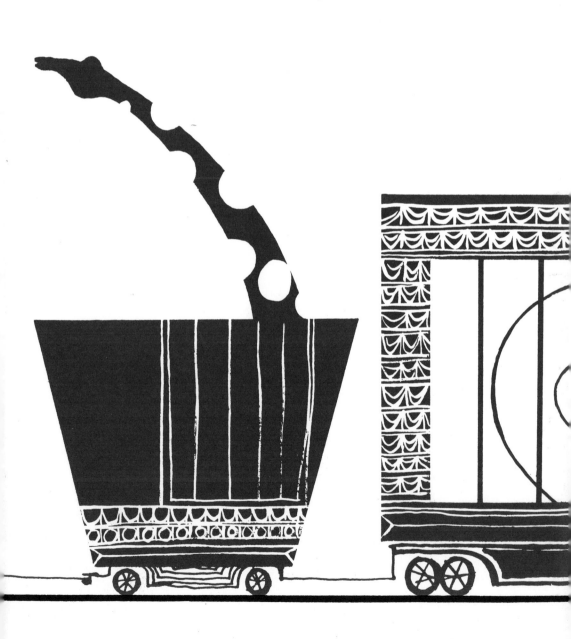

At a freight yard in a big city, another diesel took over.

The animals were safe and warm now.

Little **PUFF** headed back home, **PUFF**ing louder than ever.

Something important had happened to him at last!

Published in the United States of America in 2015 by
Universe Publishing, a division of
Rizzoli International Publications, Inc.
300 Park Avenue South
New York, NY 10010
www.rizzoliusa.com

First published in 1960 by Pantheon Books, Inc.
© 1960, 2015 William Wondriska

2015 2016 2017 2018 2019 / 10 9 8 7 6 5 4 3 2 1

Printed in China

ISBN-13: 978-0-7893-2911-0
Library of Congress Catalog Control Number: 2014914584

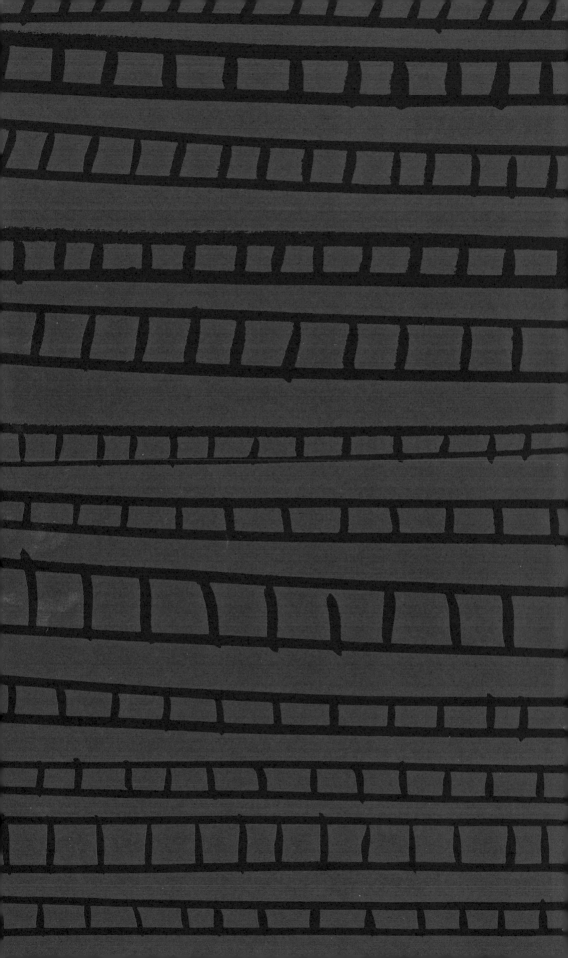